A Snowfall In Berlin

Don Nigro

A Samuel French Acting Edition

SAMUEL FRENCH

FOUNDED 1830

SAMUELFRENCH.COM
SAMUELFRENCH-LONDON.CO.UK

FOR PRODUCTION ENQUIRIES

UNITED STATES AND CANADA
Info@SamuelFrench.com
1-866-598-8449

UNITED KINGDOM AND EUROPE
Plays@SamuelFrench-London.co.uk
020-7255-4302

Each title is subject to availability from Samuel French, depending upon country of performance. Please be aware that *A SNOWFALL IN BERLIN* may not be licensed by Samuel French in your territory. Professional and amateur producers should contact the nearest Samuel French office or licensing partner to verify availability.

A SNOWFALL IN BERLIN was first produced by the Nylon Fusion Theatre Company in LATEA in New York City on March 12, 2014 with the following cast:

NATASHA. . . . . Tatyana Kot
ROSA. . . . . .Brandi Bravo
MEGAN . . . . Stephanie Heitman
EMILIA . . . . .Jessica Vera*
MULLIGAN. . . . . Don Carter*
COATES. . . . . Eric Percival
Director . . . . Shaun Peknic, SDC
Stage Manager . . . . .Laura Hirschberg*
Sound Designer . . . . .Andy Evan Cohen
Set Designer. . . . . Cassie Dorland
Lighting Designer . . . . .Wilburn Bonnell
Costume Designer . . . . .Debbi Hobson
Graphic Designer. . . . . Greg Kanyicska
Publicity . . . . Bunch Of People Press

Courtesy of Actors' Equity Association

CHARACTERS

NATASHA, Russian, a director (37)

EMILIA, Italian, her assistant (42)

COATES, British, a screenwriter (43)

ROSA, Mexican, an actress (25)

MEGAN, Irish, her friend (25)

MULLIGAN, a police detective (44)

SETTING

New York City in the present, and Berlin, some years earlier. One unit set upon which all locations are present at once. A table and some chairs. A tub. A few steps and platforms. The action is fluid like a nightmare, or a montage of old movie footage. All the players remain onstage throughout. When not directly involved in scenes they observe, relate quietly to each other, or, as scripted, comment. They are always in character and never frozen. There are no breaks between scenes. The action is continuous.

The music is Chopin's Prelude #4, Opus 28, in E-minor, and also a brief practice room musical palimpsest of overlapping fragments of Beethoven, Bach, Vivaldi, Verdi, Puccini and a very unfortunate piano. Note: under no circumstances should a real piano be harmed in the creation of this sound. Objects are alive. There are gods in all things. But especially in pianos.

For Tatyana Kot.

1.

God Collaborates

(We've been listening to Chopin's Prelude, Opus 28, #4, in E-minor, as house lights come down, but now we begin to hear other instruments joining in, playing snatches of Beethoven, Bach, Vivaldi. Pianos, violins, cellos, French horns, human voices singing Verdi and Puccini, until the growing din climaxes in the sound of a piano being chopped up by an ax, then sudden silence, and all we can hear is the whirring sound of an old film projector as lights, flickering at first like an old movie, come up on **NATASHA**, *center. At the table down right,* **EMILIA** *is laying out a game of solitaire, and* **COATES**, *facing downstage, is typing on a laptop and drinking. In the tub, up right,* **ROSA**. *Sitting on the steps, up left,* **MEGAN**. *Standing down left,* **MULLIGAN**, *looking at* **NATASHA**. *The skittering sound of film through a projector has turned into distant subway clatter.)*

NATASHA. The night she died, it was snowing. We'd spent most of the day shooting in an abandoned subway station.

ROSA. She descended into Hell.

(Sound of water dripping.)

NATASHA. You could hear water dripping somewhere.

EMILIA. Ophelia.

NATASHA. And the underworld shaking as trains passed through tunnels somewhere nearby.

(Sound of a subway train passing, then gone.)

MEGAN. Anna Karenina.

NATASHA. You find things, you use them. Edvard Munch left his paintings out in the rain. He called it collaborating with God. Everything matters. Everything is a symbol of something. Everything is patterns. The patterns are everywhere. You don't know where they're going to happen and then suddenly you see them. They've always been there but they don't exist until you see them. Things connect you couldn't have imagined would connect. Something shifts in your head, and you see the connections. But there are always scenes missing. And you need to know what to leave out. Or make it look like you intended to leave them out. God collaborates. The mistakes are where you find the truth.

COATES. Dead men's fingers.

*(**COATES** closes the laptop and drinks.)*

MULLIGAN. So we have a dead girl, drowned in a bathtub. The coroner says she'd been drinking, and she'd taken more sleeping pills than she should have, but not enough to kill her. It's possible that she lost consciousness and drowned. Or that her intention was to end her life.

ROSA. Those are pearls that were my eyes.

NATASHA. What difference does it make? She's gone. There's nothing we can do to bring her back. We've been over all this. I don't understand why you're still here.

MULLIGAN. I expect, making films, you learn to rely on your instincts.

NATASHA. You need good instincts to start with. And experience helps develop them. But you're always, to some extent, groping around in the dark.

EMILIA. The Devil lives in the closet, in the last circle of Hell.

MULLIGAN. That's how it is in my profession, too. You learn to trust your instincts. And mine tell me something's not right here.

NATASHA. Of course something's not right. A gentle, lovely child is dead. Why can't we just let her rest?

MULLIGAN. I suppose you'll be shutting down production now?

NATASHA. We're not shutting down anything. We'll keep going.

MEGAN. I know her lines.

ROSA. Megan knows my lines.

NATASHA. You think that's cold? You have your work to do. We have ours.

MULLIGAN. That's not for me to judge.

NATASHA. But you do judge. You think someone killed her. One of us. You think one of us killed her, don't you?

MULLIGAN. I think something was going on here that I don't understand. I need to understand.

NATASHA. Sometimes, you know, Detective, the most disturbing thing about looking for the truth is that you find it.

COATES. Or it finds you.

EMILIA. All the rivers of guilt flow here.

ROSA. I am the naked girl who lives in your brain.

2.

I Am The Naked Girl Who Lives In Your Brain

MULLIGAN. Tell me about the night she died.

NATASHA. I've told you this.

MULLIGAN. Tell me again.

EMILIA. He does a lot of takes. Just like you. He's waiting for that apparently random, magical accident when something unexpected is revealed.

ROSA. Chance. Chaos.

NATASHA. She was supposed to return to the set after a short break. She was late. I came to look for her. I found her dead in the tub.

ROSA. Death. Nothingness.

MULLIGAN. What happened before she took her bath?

EMILIA. She took off her clothes. Rosa preferred to bathe naked.

COATES. She was very beautiful naked.

MULLIGAN. You saw her naked?

COATES. We all saw her naked. On the set. In the film. Natasha likes everybody naked but her. It's a power thing.

EMILIA. She was a lovely child. A person wanted to mother her. Natasha wanted to mother her. Even I wanted to mother her.

ROSA. I have no mother. I have no father. I have no children. I have come here from an imaginary location.

EMILIA. I can't have children, myself. And I don't trust cats. They know something, and they won't tell.

NATASHA. Do you have children, Detective?

MULLIGAN. I have a daughter.

EMILIA. *(Turning up a card.)* Queen of Spades. Bad luck.

MULLIGAN. What happened earlier that day?

NATASHA. We'd been shooting since dawn. She was tired. She went back to the brownstone to take a bath.

MEGAN. She took a lot of baths.

EMILIA. She was a very clean girl.

COATES. She always smelled clean.

MULLIGAN. So you all live together?

MEGAN. Natasha rented a brownstone when we started, and we all moved in. Like a family, sort of.

EMILIA. The Addams family. The Borgias.

COATES. I have been engaged to appear in the pivotal role of the lecherous father.

NATASHA. Will you have some respect? She's dead. Rosa is dead.

ROSA. Yes. I'm dead. Have some respect.

MULLIGAN. Did she seem upset?

NATASHA. No more than usual.

COATES. She was a little highly strung. A bit fragile.

MEGAN. He likes them fragile. Broken. He likes them broken. And if they're not broken, he breaks them.

COATES. The broken ones think you can fix them.

MULLIGAN. Why would she take sleeping pills if you weren't done shooting for the day?

NATASHA. She had trouble sleeping. She was always tired.

EMILIA. Natasha likes to work until everybody falls over dead. It was hard on the girl.

NATASHA. You don't get anything done if you don't work.

EMILIA. And work keeps you from thinking.

MULLIGAN. How long had she been having trouble sleeping?

NATASHA. As long as we knew her.

MEGAN. But especially lately.

MULLIGAN. Was something in particular bothering her?

MEGAN. Making a film was a lot of pressure for somebody like her to handle.

MULLIGAN. So she was a troubled person.

NATASHA. A lot of people can't sleep. I can't sleep. She was nervous and sensitive. Sometimes the qualities that make a person compelling on film also make for a difficult life.

MULLIGAN. Did she have a difficult life?

MEGAN. She was an orphan. She grew up in foster homes.

ROSA. Hell is the inability to love.

MULLIGAN. Who was the last person she spoke to?

EMILIA. She made a phone call. Or got a phone call. I heard her talking in the bathroom when I went home to change.

MULLIGAN. You don't know who she was talking to?

COATES. She was probably talking to herself. She did that quite a bit.

ROSA. I'm cold.

EMILIA. Sometimes she called people in the middle of the night. I don't know who, because she didn't seem to have many friends in the city. Maybe she just called random numbers. I've done that.

ROSA. Natasha is cold.

NATASHA. She got lonely. She was a child. Afraid of the dark.

ROSA. Valentina is cold.

MEGAN. It was me. She was talking to me. I mean, she called me that night. I might not have been the only person she called, I don't know.

MULLIGAN. What did you talk about?

3.

Sorry, Wrong Number

(A telephone conversation.)

MEGAN. Hello?

ROSA. Valentina?

MEGAN. Rosa?

ROSA. Is that you?

MEGAN. This is Megan. Who else would it be?

ROSA. I don't know. This isn't me.

MEGAN. Who is Valentina?

ROSA. Who is this really?

MEGAN. It's Megan.

ROSA. If you're Megan then who am I?

MEGAN. You're Rosa.

ROSA. I don't think so.

MEGAN. Have you been drinking?

ROSA. I don't remember. Are you sure it's me? Because it doesn't sound like me. Of course, it never sounds like me. That's how I know I'm not here. If it sounds like me, it must be somebody else.

MEGAN. Honey, is something wrong?

ROSA. No. Everything is wonderful. Natasha says I'm going to be brilliant. I don't know when that's supposed to happen. Not today. I think she has me confused with somebody who lives in her head. And I don't want to live in Natasha's head. It's a very scary place, inside her head. There's water dripping in there, and a baby crying in another room, and somebody's chopping up a piano with an ax. Why did you call me?

MEGAN. I didn't call you. You called me.

ROSA. I'm sorry. I think you have the wrong number. I was calling Valentina.

MEGAN. I don't know who that is.

ROSA. I was hoping you could tell me. Do you want to go to a movie?

MEGAN. No, I don't want to go to a movie. I'm in a movie. And so are you.

ROSA. All right. But I need to take a bath first.

COATES. You don't need to take a bath. You're always very clean. You smell like clean laundry. And you squeak when I rub my fingers on you. I like things that squeak. Except for mice. I don't like mice.

MEGAN. Who's that? Is somebody else there?

ROSA. I feel dirty. Coates always makes me feel dirty. It's one of his special talents. It must be really dirty in England. I wish I was there now. But only if Coates was someplace else.

COATES. I am someplace else. I've always been someplace else. I am entirely a figment of your imagination.

ROSA. Don't come in.

MEGAN. Who are you talking to?

ROSA. I thought it was Valentina, but apparently not, because you don't sound like her at all. Unless I'm Valentina. Maybe it's just because I have a cold. What number was I calling?

MEGAN. You were calling me.

ROSA. Well, that's all right. I'll try again later.

MEGAN. Rosa, I'm coming over there right now, okay?

ROSA. No. Don't come here. Because I'm not here now. Plus I'm naked. And I'm wet. I'll meet you there.

MEGAN. Where?

ROSA. I don't know. You'll recognize me when you don't see me. I'll be the girl who isn't there. Just be careful. I've had a premonition that something terrible is going to happen. I dozed off for a minute in the bath and saw it in my dream. There was a man with a monkey.

COATES. Green tea. The creature follows along the top of the wall, grinning at me.

ROSA. And when you take a bath, be sure and wash every part of your body. Because men are the enemy, and men are horribly filthy creatures, like monkeys, and if we're dirty too, then how will God be able to tell us apart, when he's sending all the men to Hell? Except, of course, that the men have penises. At least, all the ones I've met so far.

NATASHA. Cut.

ROSA. Coates has a penis.

MEGAN. Coates is a penis.

EMILIA. Leonardo da Vinci had a penis. He used to paint with it.

NATASHA. CUT.

ROSA. Natasha doesn't have a penis. I know because one night when it was storming I—

NATASHA. I said CUT, damn it. Cut when I tell you to cut.

ROSA. We're sorry. Your call could not be completed as dialed. Please try again after you're dead.

4.

Detective, Would You Like Some Wieners?

MEGAN. And when I got there, I saw an ambulance and police cars and they told me she was dead.

MULLIGAN. Did you often get strange phone calls from her?

MEGAN. Not as strange as that one.

MULLIGAN. Who is this Valentina she was talking about?

MEGAN. I have no idea.

MULLIGAN. And you thought you heard her talking to someone else?

EMILIA. Detective, would you like some wieners?

NATASHA. Why are you offering him wieners?

EMILIA. I thought this was where I was supposed to offer him the wieners.

COATES. Dead men's fingers.

NATASHA. How much have you had to drink?

EMILIA. Did we cut the wieners?

NATASHA. There never were any wieners.

EMILIA. *(Showing her the script.)* But it's right here in the script. Look. "Detective, would you like some wieners?"

NATASHA. Let me see that.

EMILIA. I knew I remembered wieners.

NATASHA. This is not what I wrote.

COATES. You're not writing the script. I am.

NATASHA. We're collaborating.

COATES. Maybe you are. I'm not.

EMILIA. But she is the great directrix. She creates the film like God created New Jersey. If you happened to scribble a few words down before we began shooting, it's simply grist for her creative process, to be absorbed into her creation once she and her lover, the camera, begin the real work. Do not imagine that you are the author of this film, just because you wrote it.

COATES. Well, I'm not the author of the line, "Detective, would you like some wieners?"

NATASHA. If you didn't write it, and I didn't write it, who did?

EMILIA. It must have been God, collaborating. We've got to stop him before he collaborates again. Every time God collaborates, somebody dies.

MULLIGAN. I really don't care who put in the wieners. This is not about wieners.

EMILIA. Everything is about wieners.

NATASHA. Emilia has had too much too drink. She doesn't know what she's saying.

COATES. She doesn't know what she's saying when she's sober.

EMILIA. I know exactly what I'm saying. And I'm never sober. What am I saying?

MULLIGAN. I just want to understand what happened to this girl.

COATES. The truth is, Rosa had been having emotional problems for some time. Some people just didn't want to see it.

MEGAN. But you saw it, didn't you? That's exactly what you look for in a woman, because that's the kind you can prey on, like a hyena.

COATES. Hyenas are important animals in the food chain. Scavengers are necessary to pick off the small and the weak. It's called thinning the herd. I direct you to page sixty-nine of the Predator's Handbook, where it clearly explains that each potential victim has an area of most intense vulnerability, and the trick is to find it, save the knowledge until you need it, then use it. The flaw in your beloved is your ally. It's your way in. And it will lead her to cherish what is least worth loving in you.

And when you put your finger on it, she will tremble helplessly under your hand. And she did.

MULLIGAN. You were having a relationship with the dead girl?

COATES. Well, in my defense, she wasn't dead then.

MULLIGAN. Were all of you aware this was going on?

EMILIA. I'm not aware of anything. I'm Italian.

NATASHA. I don't keep track of who's sleeping with who. My relations with the cast are strictly professional. Not that I wasn't fond of her. She was a lovely girl, but lost.

5.

City Of Dreadful Night

ROSA. I came to New York to study acting. I grew up in foster homes. I had nobody. I wanted a fresh start. I had so many hopes when I got here. But I hated acting school. Acting is this. No, acting is that. This system. No, that system. This teacher is God. No, this teacher is God, that teacher is the Devil. Worship me. No, worship me. They smile and cut your throat. It all seemed so unhealthy to me. I thought if I just got out there and started working, everything would be all right. So I dropped out and began auditioning. But there were so many things they wouldn't even consider me for because of my accent.

COATES. Americans have no taste and very tiny brains. They believe they're the only people on earth without an accent. When Americans speak English it's like dogs barking.

ROSA. And my hair. In American culture, there is no such thing as a blond Hispanic girl. So I couldn't get roles because I had a Spanish accent, and I couldn't get Hispanic roles because my hair was the wrong color. So I dyed my hair, but then I was just a girl with dyed hair and an accent. I was running out of money. I wasn't eating. I was just at the edge of the abyss, looking down into the water. I went to a diner, late at night, and ordered some soup. I didn't have enough to pay, but my friend Megan worked there, and usually she'd find a way to get me something to eat.

MEGAN. I'm always the best friend.

ROSA. But Megan was off that night, and when the manager realized I didn't have any money, he said he was going to call the police. And I started to cry. And a couple of tables over, there was this beautiful Russian woman, arguing with an Italian woman about something. And she looked over and saw me crying, and how the manager was treating me, and Natasha just jumped right out of her seat, like a lioness defending her cub. She scared the hell out of the manager, bought me dinner, and listened to my story. She was so kind to me. And she said to Emilia, right then and there—

NATASHA. This is her. This is the girl in the tub. You see? Random events. God collaborates.

ROSA. I had no idea what she was talking about, and it crossed my mind for a second or two that I'd fallen into the hands of a dangerous lunatic, but I didn't care. She was so wonderful. And they took me in. And gave me a place to stay. And the next day we were shooting the movie. It was all like a dream. Natasha is like a dream.

6.

The Lady From Shanghai

NATASHA. Everything is a movie. You're the star of your own movie and a featured player in other people's and an extra in most. But if you just embrace the reality that everything is a movie, then no amount of suffering or humiliation can ever be entirely without meaning. It's just necessary for the movie God is directing. And that God is himself entirely imaginary is not a problem, because he's a character in his own movie, directed by another God who is a character in turn in another movie. It's all movies, all an infinite series of interpenetrating movies, like a set of Russian dolls, one inside the other, or mirrors reflecting mirrors. The trick is to understand what movie you're in. If you think you're in one movie, and you're actually in another one, a person can get killed.

MULLIGAN. Is that what happened to Rosa? Did she end up in the wrong movie?

NATASHA. Rosa took too many sleeping pills and drowned.

MULLIGAN. So you think she was trying to kill herself?

NATASHA. No. I don't think she'd do that. I think it was an accident. She lost count of how many pills she'd taken. She was a very appealing girl, but disorganized. Her life was chaotic. I was trying to teach her to be more careful. About organizing her life. About priorities. About men. She had rather poor judgement about men.

COATES. For which, on behalf of my entire sex, I would just like to express my gratitude.

MULLIGAN. I expect your life is very well organized. You're careful. You pay careful attention to detail in your work.

NATASHA. If you're not careful, you die. You die anyway. But if you're not careful, you die sooner.

MULLIGAN. And do you have good judgement about men?

NATASHA. No.

COATES. Fear death by water.

NATASHA. Do you have a close relationship with your daughter, Detective?

MULLIGAN. No. I don't.

NATASHA. Do you want to?

MULLIGAN. What I want has nothing to do with it. She liked me a great deal when she was a little girl. Now she never calls me. She won't answer my letters. She won't tell me why. I suppose I've done something wrong, but I don't know what it is.

NATASHA. You spend your life solving puzzles, but this is a puzzle nobody can solve: people stop loving you.

MULLIGAN. I have a recurring nightmare that I'm looking for a missing person, and midway in the investigation I discover that it's my daughter. I follow her into a room full of mirrors. It's like a funhouse, with a million reflected images. And I can't tell which one is real.

COATES. For death remembered should be like a mirror.

MEGAN. *The Lady From Shanghai*. The mirror scene at the end. He shoots into the mirrors.

NATASHA. I like you better than I thought I would. But it's a trick, isn't it? You tell me a personal story that for all I know you've just made up on the spot, so that I'll open up to you in return.

MULLIGAN. Do you think everything's a trick?

NATASHA. I think what anything appears to mean depends on where you put the camera. What is it? What are you looking at?

MULLIGAN. A woman with a secret.

NATASHA. The premise of a very large number of movies, mostly bad ones.

MULLIGAN. But this is not a movie.

NATASHA. Are you absolutely certain? Only a fool is certain, in life or in art. Some people demand certainty in art because they find so little of it in their lives, except for death, which seems unreal until it happens, and then seems so real it's the most unreal thing of all. Maybe it's a movie about a police detective who doesn't realize he's in a movie. We think we want certainty, but certainty is a lie. We live most of our lives almost completely submerged in a sea of ambiguity. We don't really know the people we think we love. We can't trust the people we think love us. They keep changing. Their faces keep changing. But the movie goes on, and we can't stop the film.

EMILIA. We can always burn down the theatre.

(EMILIA *drinks.*)

7.

Laura

*(**MULLIGAN** at the table. **MEGAN** is the waitress.)*

MEGAN. So, did you come here because you want to question me away from the set, or have you fallen desperately in love with me?

MULLIGAN. I came here for the pie.

MEGAN. The pie is terrible.

MULLIGAN. I'm an American. I have no taste and a tiny little brain. What are you doing working in here? I thought you were an actress.

MEGAN. This is independent film. If we're lucky, we make enough for bus fare to a real job.

MULLIGAN. You were in the movie before Rosa?

MEGAN. I was up for her part, but Natasha wasn't satisfied. Then she came in here and took one look at Rosa and I was playing the best friend. I'm always the best friend. Which is ironic because I have no friends. Except for Rosa, and she's dead. Maybe it's dangerous to be my friend. Better keep your distance.

MULLIGAN. It didn't bother you that Rosa got the part?

MEGAN. I was happy for her. One minute she was starving, and the next thing she knew, she had plenty to eat, a nice place to stay, and the lead in a movie. Lucky girl. For a while.

EMILIA. The Queen of Spades.

MULLIGAN. So with Rosa gone, do you get her part?

MEGAN. Natasha hasn't decided yet. Do you think that's why I killed her?

MULLIGAN. I don't know. Is it?

MEGAN. If you're not in love with me, you're in love with somebody. You have that look a man gets when he finds himself in a situation he can't control. This is how women get black eyes.

MULLIGAN. You've made a study of this, have you?

MEGAN. I minored in abnormal psychology.

MULLIGAN. You think I'm abnormal?

MEGAN. All men are abnormal. Love is abnormal. Emilia says you've been looking at the scenes we shot with Rosa over and over again. It's hard to take your eyes off her, isn't it? I know what it is. It's *Laura.*

MULLIGAN. Laura who?

MEGAN. The movie, *Laura.* Don't you know it?

MULLIGAN. I don't go to the movies much.

MEGAN. Mulligan, what do you do when you're off duty, except come in here and accuse me of murder? Never mind. I probably don't want to know. There's this dead girl in a painting, in the movie, *Laura,* and the detective investigating falls hopelessly in love with her.

MULLIGAN. With a dead girl in a painting?

MEGAN. That's what it is. You're in love with a dead girl. People always fell in love with Rosa. She was that sort of girl. You couldn't help it.

MULLIGAN. Were you in love with her?

MEGAN. Everybody was.

MULLIGAN. Except the person who killed her.

MEGAN. Especially the person who killed her. You don't like movies but you sit and stare at the same footage over and over again, all night. You're in love, all right.

MULLIGAN. I'm looking for something.

MEGAN. What is it?

MULLIGAN. I'll know when I find it.

MEGAN. Or maybe you're in love with Natasha. Everybody's always in love with her, too. It must be a terrible pain in the ass, to have everybody always in love with you.

MULLIGAN. Isn't everybody in love with you?

MEGAN. Just the bastards.

MULLIGAN. What do you do when you're off duty?

MEGAN. Are you asking me out?

MULLIGAN. I'm asking you what you do when you're off duty.

MEGAN. When I'm off duty I step through the looking glass and into Natasha's movie.

MULLIGAN. And when you're not doing that?

MEGAN. I sit at home and watch movies in the dark. I'm looking for something. Listen, just between us Irish. These people. They can be very seductive. But they can't be trusted. They're not like you.

MULLIGAN. No, they're a lot prettier.

MEGAN. I'm trying to tell you something. You think you're the tough guy, but you're out of your depth here. This is not your world. In this world, you are the innocent. These people are like the movies. They get into your brain, and you can't get them out. The manager's glaring at me like a constipated troll. You better leave me a good tip.

MULLIGAN. Here's a tip. Get out of the movie business. You might end up dead in a bathtub.

MEGAN. Maybe I want to end up dead in a bathtub. Maybe Rosa did, too.

MULLIGAN. Make up your mind. Do you think she was murdered, or do you think she wanted to die?

MEGAN. Maybe both. Either way, these people killed her. I don't know exactly how. But they killed her. Make them pay. But not until we're done shooting the movie. First I want to be a star. Then they can kill me, too.

(She turns and goes.)

8.

Vertigo

COATES. That's very American of you, to still be lurking about where you aren't welcome and don't belong. Americans believe in their hearts that God has given them the world and all living things on it to fuck up any way they please.

MULLIGAN. Just what is your problem? Why do you have this thing about Americans?

COATES. I don't have a thing. I feel no differently about Americans than I would about any herd of violent, bigoted, Bible-thumping, feeble-minded, foul smelling, fat-assed, lip-diddling, slack-jawed cretins.

MULLIGAN. You better watch out, pal.

COATES. Watch out? What should I watch out for? Isn't this the land of the free? Just because I can't help observing that your people are a couple of rungs below spider monkeys on the evolutionary ladder, that doesn't give you the right to threaten me.

MULLIGAN. I'm not threatening you. I'm warning you to be careful how you speak to a police officer.

COATES. I stand warned. Although I would prefer to sit warned, if you don't mind. Standing warned is hard on my knees, and I've spent a lot of time on my knees, worshipping the Snow Queen.

(Sits at the table, pours a drink.)

I can't help it if I'm trapped in this vulgar, money-grubbing, gun-worshipping, hypocritical sewer of a country. And the worst thing is, it's contagious. Stupidity is actually contagious here. It's worse than venereal disease. And I'm starting to lose my accent. I now apparently speak a bastard form of pigeon English.

And American movies are the most worthless idiotic excrement on the face of the earth.

MULLIGAN. And here you are, making one.

COATES. It's true. I have fallen far beneath my station. You don't seem to appreciate what a significant figure I am, back in the civilized world, where at least thirty percent of the population can read the back of their cornflakes box. In Britain, I have been quite a celebrated playwright, which is to say, in order to make a living, I write movies. I am a serious artist, which in America means that I am patronized by cretins and plagiarized by vermin. The movies at home are stupid enough, I'll grant you, and abysmally dull, but nothing can match the obscenely expensive, relentlessly juvenile and borderline subhuman drivel they manufacture in this particular circle of Hell.

MULLIGAN. Then what are you doing here?

COATES. Dying. I am dying, Egypt. My life is a charnel house. I scuttle like rats over piles of old bones.

(*He drinks.*)

I came here for the money, and as soon as I got here, I realized what a terrible mistake I'd made, but every time I go to the airport, I have a panic attack. The world spins, and I have horrendous dreams of falling from a great height, like Kim Novak in *Vertigo,* or Satan, into the ocean. And then deep into the water. Into everlasting darkness. With those that God forgot.

MULLIGAN. But you can't be making much of anything on this film. So why are you here? Why aren't you out in Hollywood making some real money?

NATASHA. A set of Russian dolls. Each universe nested inside another.

COATES. Natasha. Natasha is the answer. I couldn't resist her. Nobody can. Natasha is the ultimate challenge for a man like me. Incredibly sexy. Smoldering eyes. Clearly, fire inside. And yet touch her and she goes as rigid as a frozen squirrel. She will not let me in. Figuratively and literally. She drives me completely out of my mind. And she enjoys it. I won't say she does it deliberately, but she knows it's happening, and she takes a sort of dark pleasure in it. It's some manner of deeply twisted revenge, I think.

MULLIGAN. Revenge for what?

COATES. Who knows? Women are always punishing some poor schmuck for something the last man did to them. But this one has turned it into art. For her, everything's a movie. She's a natural in front of the camera, too. She can cry on cue. Which leads one to ask, are any of her emotions real? She could be so good at it that she even fools herself. What does it matter, if she gets what she wants? And she always gets what she wants. We need rain in this scene. Cue the rain. And it rains. She is the Queen of the Rainy Country. Don't be misled by her charms. She is very angry. Or very guilty. Or both. The most dangerous creature on the face of the earth is a woman who's been wounded. Utterly ruthless. So don't tell me to watch out, pal. You watch out. Don't say I didn't warn you. You stand warned.

(He drinks.)

9.

The Creature From The Black Lagoon

NATASHA. In my dream I'm making my way home through heavy snowfall. The streetcars aren't running, and I'm cold and tired from walking through snowdrifts, but the world is beautiful when all the dirt is covered up with snow, and I'm comforted by the thought that when I get there I can go upstairs and run myself a warm bath. When I get home, the house is quiet. I can just hear the ticking of my father's clocks in the parlor, and from upstairs, the sound of water dripping. And I am possessed, suddenly, by an overwhelming feeling of dread, a premonition that something terrible has happened. I run up the steps, my heart pounding. I can hardly breathe.

ROSA. I want to go home and take a bath. I feel dirty.

NATASHA. We need to work tonight.

ROSA. Can't we take at least one night off? I'm so tired.

NATASHA. Everybody gets tired. Mediocre people stop. The obsessed keep going. An artist must be as relentlessly obsessed as the ticking of God's clockworks.

ROSA. But we work and work and you're never satisfied.

NATASHA. We can be satisfied when we're dead. Until then, we work until we get it right. Emilia, will you get rid of that drink?

EMILIA. Yes, Captain Ahab.

(**EMILIA** *downs the drink in one gulp.*)

NATASHA. We're way behind schedule. Let's pick it up from the bathtub scene.

MULLIGAN. So this movie is about a group of exiles who come together to make a film about a girl who dies in a bathtub.

COATES. It's the Tower of Babel. We are a confusion of tongues, all jabbering at once, like the Devil's orchestra tuning up in Hell, and nobody can comprehend anybody else.

MULLIGAN. You're making a film about a girl who dies in a bathtub, when the girl in the film who dies in a bathtub actually dies in a bathtub.

EMILIA. Except that now it's become a film about a film in which a girl who dies in a bathtub actually dies in a bathtub while making a film about a girl who dies in a bathtub. I don't even know what I'm saying any more.

COATES. She'd film actors being murdered if she could get away with it. And to be fair, what difference does it make if a few actors get killed? There's too damned many of them running around anyway. You never run out of actors. Only money and time.

MULLIGAN. Who came up with the idea of the girl dying in the tub?

COATES. The Empress of All the Russians.

NATASHA. I did not. It was your idea.

COATES. Typical Soviet revisionist history. I was throwing ideas at her helter-skelter in a desperate attempt to come up with something so clever she'd sleep with me, and that one seemed to strike a chord in her.

MULLIGAN. But where did you get that particular idea?

COATES. Only God knows, and he went down with the Titanic. Stole it from somewhere or other. Ninety percent of all movies are stolen from other movies. Give me eleven or twelve years and it will come to me. All past knowledge swirls in the maelstrom of the water closet of my brain.

MULLIGAN. And in the movie, who actually does kill the girl?

COATES. There are multiple drafts with mutually incompatible outcomes. The Siberian Goddess has not yet decided which unsatisfactory alternative will have the dubious honor of becoming our group hallucination. She prefers that the ending of the film be revealed to her when we get there by some prehistoric swamp demon who whispers in her ear. Like the Creature from the Black Lagoon.

MULLIGAN. So none of you actually has any idea how the movie is supposed to turn out?

EMILIA. This is why I drink. That, and the fact that the miniature people who live in my doll house want to get out. They've been on the phone a lot. I'm worried they're calling in air strikes.

NATASHA. Emilia.

EMILIA. At night I watch them have sex. They make these little squeaking sounds. Like carnivorous mice.

NATASHA. Will you shut up?

EMILIA. Don't tell me to shut up. I am a woman who has studied the copulation of hieroglyphics with Eisenstein. I've done naked trampoline with Otto Preminger. I had a three way with the Lumiere brothers. And I picked you up out of the gutter when you were nothing. So who the hell are you to tell me to shut up?

NATASHA. All right. Let's take a break.

   (NATASHA *walks away.*)

EMILIA. I've hurt her feelings. Every once in a while, inexplicably, a random shot gets through her defenses and I feel like dying.

10.

A Snowfall In Berlin

(**EMILIA** *retreats to a corner to brood.* **MULLIGAN** *follows.* **NATASHA** *has sat down upstage, as if at the base of a wall.*)

MULLIGAN. You're her assistant director.

EMILIA. Yes. That is my current definition. It's a great honor.

MULLIGAN. But you're also in the film.

EMILIA. We're all in the film.

MULLIGAN. Coates wrote the screenplay, but he's also in the film.

EMILIA. Everybody is in the film. Even you are in the film.

MULLIGAN. I don't think so.

EMILIA. You don't think so, but you are. You'll see.

MULLIGAN. And you're all from different countries. Natasha's Russian. Coates is British. You're from Italy. Megan's Irish. Rosa was Mexican.

EMILIA. Yes. We're all exiles here. Strangers in an increasingly strange land, gathered into the arms of the goddess. That's what Natasha does. She rescues orphans. She tries to create a little family around her, out of the discarded fragments of other people's lives. She mothers compulsively. The problem is, she's not very good at it.

MULLIGAN. You're very angry at her.

EMILIA. Never presume to know the ultimate truth about any human soul. The heart of another is a dark forest. Russian proverb.

MULLIGAN. What did you mean about picking her up out of the gutter?

EMILIA. I found her in the street, like a stray cat. Berlin was the place to be, if you were a young filmmaker, or any sort of artist. I was walking home late at night from shooting a film in an abandoned building. It was snowing, and I was cold and discouraged, because it wasn't going well, and I didn't know how to fix it. And I saw her sitting at the base of a wall, all huddled up, with her red hair streaming down over her face. I tried to just walk by. You see people in the street. You feel bad for them, but what can you do? You can't help everybody, especially if you have next to nothing yourself. You put your head down and just keep walking. But she seemed so lost, like a creature out of some fairy tale. Of course, in fairy tales a person often lives to regret rescuing such a creature. You bring them home and they end up eating the baby. I thought of the story my grandmother told about her father driving his wagon home one dark night and finding a white bundle at the center of a crossroads, and how he thought it must be an abandoned child, so he stopped and picked up the bundle, but when he saw what it was, he threw it down in the road as hard as he could and drove away. It was a changeling, a demon child. My brain told me to just keep walking, but I found myself turning around and going back. It was one of those moments when you observe yourself doing something without really knowing you were going to do it, but once you're doing it, it seems inevitable, as if somebody else is operating your body. As if your life were a movie, and you're trapped inside the frames. You want to act differently but you can't. So I walked back to her in the snow, and asked her if she was all right.

NATASHA. Yes.

EMILIA. Are you sure?

NATASHA. No.

EMILIA. And then she looked up at me, and I saw her eyes.

NATASHA. *(Looking up at her.)* I don't know what I am.

EMILIA. She was so beautiful I couldn't breathe. And her eyes were like nobody else's eyes. Like the eyes of some creature from another world. You're going to freeze to death out here, I said.

NATASHA. Yes.

EMILIA. Don't you have some place to go?

NATASHA. No.

EMILIA. You sound Russian. Are you Russian?

NATASHA. I'm from Siberia. We're familiar with the cold.

EMILIA. I'm from Italy. We're familiar with everything. What are you doing in Berlin?

NATASHA. I came here to be a dancer. I had an audition today, but I was so weak from hunger I could barely stand up, and the snow was falling, and I was so tired, I just wanted to lie down in the snow and go to sleep.

EMILIA. Would you like some soup? You need something warm inside you.

COATES. Yes, she does, but it's not soup.

EMILIA. You shut up. I'm telling this. You weren't there.

NATASHA. I don't want to be where I don't belong.

EMILIA. What choice do you have? Nobody belongs anywhere. Exiles need to take care of each other. Yes?

NATASHA. Yes. Thank you.

EMILIA. And so I took the beautiful green eyed stranger home with me, and heated up some soup, and gave her some green tea, and we sat by the fire and talked, and as she warmed up, her face began to glow, and her hair was curling from the moisture in it, and she looked at me like some sad, lost young animal, and my heart went out to her, and I let her spend the night, and we've been together ever since.

MULLIGAN. But you were the filmmaker. She was a dancer. And now she's the director. How did that happen?

EMILIA. I made the mistake of feeling sorry for her. She'd come to Berlin to be a dancer, but she had no friends there, no connections, and she'd run out of money.

She was starving to death. She was lost. She was a lost creature.

ROSA. I am the naked girl in your dream.

EMILIA. So I let her stay with me, and told her she could earn her keep by helping on the set. She could be the script girl. Go for coffee and sandwiches. And so she came. And she watched. And from the first moment she was on the set, it was like she was hypnotized. I can't describe to you the eerie sense of wonder she seemed to radiate. Her eyes were big, and excited, but she was very calm.

NATASHA. It was like I'd come home to a place I'd known in another life.

EMILIA. And this scene wasn't working.

MEGAN. This is wrong, what we're doing.

COATES. If it wasn't, what would be the point?

MEGAN. I don't like betraying people.

COATES. You'll get used to it.

MEGAN. Can we stop? This just doesn't feel right.

EMILIA. And I was frustrated and tired, and I didn't know how to fix it, and then from behind me I heard this voice.

NATASHA. Try it without the movement. Just be still. And say it with your back to him.

EMILIA. At first I dismissed it as the sort of comment an amateur makes, somebody completely out of her element. But nobody had a better idea, so we tried it, just to humor her.

MEGAN. *(Facing downstage with her back to* **COATES** *now, motionless.)* This is wrong, what we're doing.

EMILIA. And it worked. It worked really beautifully. And then she had another idea. And then another idea. And every day, as we were filming, when the actors didn't know what to do, more and more they began to look at her, instead of me. And at first we made a joke of it. About who was really directing the film.

NATASHA. There's too much light. There should be more shadows. It should happen almost but not quite in the dark.

EMILIA. But it wasn't really a joke. She didn't know anything when she started, but she was like a vacuum cleaner, sucking up information left and right, talking with the actors, the crew, asking questions, absorbing everything. Even though she was just learning the technical aspects as she went along, something in her already knew what to do.

NATASHA. It's all right not to see her face.

EMILIA. But we want to see her face.

NATASHA. Yes, and when we don't get what we want, we want it more. Just try it.

EMILIA. And she became so valuable to me that I ended up giving her assistant director credit. And on the next one we were co-directors. Then she said she'd like to try one on her own, and by that point I wasn't sure I could do without her, so I agreed to help. And I've been her assistant ever since.

MULLIGAN. And you didn't resent that? Her gradually taking over?

EMILIA. The thing is, if you are technically skilled, competent, intelligent, a hard worker, a good craftsman, and you come upon somebody who is a genius, who has things in them that you don't know where they come from, and they don't know where they come from— to watch her work, there is such beauty, it's almost a holy thing. It gives you goose bumps. It's sad, but there it is. I am competent. But she can do things I would never come up with, and make something that was dead suddenly come alive. The merely competent must have the humility to recognize that, in the end, what you create is more important than your personal vanity. Otherwise, you're not creating. You're destroying.

ROSA. We are all disposable. We can all be cut from someone else's film. Sooner or later everybody ends up on the cutting room floor.

11.

The Cutting Room Floor

NATASHA. I had a dance audition, in Berlin, and I didn't know the city well, and didn't speak the language, and I got lost, and it was snowing, and finally I found this very old building, and the lower part seemed to be abandoned, but I made my way up a dark staircase to the upper floors, where there was a music conservatory—

> *(Sound of a piano, then a violin, then a cello, a French horn, human voices singing opera, and then another piano, all different pieces, as at the beginning.)*

—and on the top floor there was a long, dark corridor with many doors, practice rooms on either side, and I could hear pianos and violins, French horns and cellos and human voices singing, all different songs, all at once, and I hadn't eaten in a long time, and the climb up the steps had made me very weak, and started to get dizzy, and I remembered my mother's piano in our house, and—

> *(The sound of a piano being chopped to pieces with an ax, a horrifying climax, as before, followed by sudden silence, with just the ticking of clocks.)*

MULLIGAN. So you rescued Rosa the way Emilia rescued you.

NATASHA. What?

MULLIGAN. You rescued Rosa the same way Emilia rescued you.

> *(The ticking of the clocks fades.)*

NATASHA. Did I?

MULLIGAN. You identified with her. Another lost girl.

NATASHA. She wasn't much like me, really. She was a girl who was afraid of everything but couldn't get enough of anything. And she was desperate to be loved, which is never a good strategy for happiness.

ROSA. Hell is the inability to love.

EMILIA. The key to happiness is the ability to perpetuate as long as possible the illusion that one is loved. When you can no longer perpetuate that illusion, you die.

NATASHA. I tried to tell her. One is either the god or the straw dog, the wanton boy or the fly, the murderer or the victim. There is no middle ground.

EMILIA. She says things she doesn't believe. It's a transparent device to protect her from her feelings, and it doesn't work.

COATES. There is no such thing as love. There is only desire, and its satisfaction or frustration.

NATASHA. Rosa was terribly insecure. A woman can't afford to be that way. She won't survive.

ROSA. Why was that waiter looking at me?

NATASHA. Nobody was looking at you.

ROSA. Everybody in the restaurant was looking at me.

NATASHA. Well, what if they were? You're beautiful. What do you want me to do about it?

ROSA. You're the director. Make them stop.

NATASHA. This is America. People can look at whoever they want to.

ROSA. I hate people looking at me.

MEGAN. They're just ordinary, nice people looking at a pretty girl.

ROSA. How do you know they're nice? People aren't nice.

MEGAN. Sometimes people are nice.

ROSA. Nobody is actually nice unless they're screwing you, or they want to.

MEGAN. That's horrible.

ROSA. I know it's horrible. The truth is horrible. Natasha taught me that.

MEGAN. If you hate being looked at, then why are you an actress?

ROSA. I'm not an actress.

MEGAN. Then what are you doing in this movie?

ROSA. I'm not in this movie. I'm on the cutting room floor.

NATASHA. Next time we'll go someplace else.

ROSA. There is no place else. The place you are is the only place. Everywhere else is just off camera. I want to go off camera. I want to disappear into the dark. Like you. You're in the dark. The director lives in the dark. Only the actors are in the light. And we're not real.

EMILIA. But you see, dear, since it's Natasha's movie, Natasha is the movie, and both are contained within her. The light and the darkness. Creation and destruction. Love and hate. Copulation and murder. She the alpha and the omega. She is the goddess, and we are all her subjects. She is the murderess and the victim.

COATES. You're completely insane, you know that? You're nuttier than a box of squirrels.

ROSA. Don't make fun of crazy people. I was in a madhouse once.

COATES. Just visiting, I hope.

ROSA. No. Not just visiting. I saw a woman in the street hitting her child, and I tried to take it away from her, and the police came, and they put me in this place. There was a man who was tormented by an invisible clown. I will stay on the moon and die with you, he said. He called me the girl in the moon. The people in there were always looking at me like they were fine, but there was something seriously wrong with me. When people look at me I feel naked.

NATASHA. The camera makes everybody naked.

EMILIA. Some more naked than others. The mistake is presuming you're the one who's crazy when maybe you're crazy but so is everybody else, so what's the difference? I was raised by nuns and everybody there was crazy. And now I can speak twelve languages in the dark, but I only understand three of them. I can play the violin, the piano, and cribbage, but my heart is like a dried pear and my brain is bleeding, and my soul is made of goat cheese.

ROSA. Sometimes I feel like I'm drowning.

NATASHA. You'll be fine. Just remember to breathe.

ROSA. When I try to breathe I drown.

NATASHA. You're thinking too much. Forget that you're making a film. Just take a deep breath, and let yourself go under. Everything interesting is beneath the surface. There is no beauty without strangeness, and whatever is strange frightens us. But all accidents are charged with meaning. Everything in a film means something, whether you wanted it to or not. The act of looking creates meaning. Experience is like a palimpsest, an imperfectly erased wax tablet. You can see through the worn away places like the holes in swiss cheese. There are layers and layers. The film draws a boundary and you look inside it, as into a mirror, and you forget who you are, you fall into the mirror, like falling into the water, and you drown in it. The secret is, don't be afraid to drown.

COATES. Like Fritz Lang's wife.

MULLIGAN. Fritz Lang's wife?

COATES. That's it. Fritz Lang's wife.

MULLIGAN. What about her?

NATASHA. Let's take it from Fritz Lang's Wife.

12.

Fritz Lang's Wife

(Sound of footsteps echoing down a long corridor.)

COATES. Fritz Lang, the great German director, with his eyepatch and his stuffed monkey, footsteps echoing down a long corridor, enters the office of Josef Goebbels, Nazi Minister of Propaganda. Animal skins on the floor. Animal heads on the walls. Smell of expensive cologne. Out the window, the hands of a big clock.

NATASHA. Sometimes I dream about Berlin.

COATES. Goebbels greets him like an old friend, seats him in a leather chair, offers him a cigar, and apologizes for confiscating his movie, explaining that unfortunately he had a few problems with the ending. The Führer should come in at the end, defeat Dr Mabuse and save the world. It's not enough that the villain goes insane. What does it prove that a person goes insane? Anybody can go insane.

ROSA. I can.

EMILIA. I can.

COATES. There is no moral lesson there. And I believe, Fritz, says Goebbels, that art must have a moral lesson. Art must uphold family values, good old fashioned conservative values. So if you could just make it a bit more uplifting, we might allow it to be released. And Fritz Lang says, as politely as he can, that he'd prefer not to.

MEGAN. Nobody leaves this movie alive.

COATES. Goebbels smiles at him. I know, Fritz, that you are a good German at heart, he says. Those ugly rumors about your Jewish grandmother could not be true. The Führer loved *Metropolis,* and *Die Nibelungen* so moved him that he sobbed in the arms of Himmler and said, at last, a man who will give us great Nazi films.

EMILIA. The Devil reflected in a copper pot.

COATES. So Fritz is drenched in sweat, thinking, Christ, he knows my grandmother was Jewish. I've got to get the hell out of here. If he'd just shut up I could run to the bank and escape to Paris. But this demented son of a bitch won't stop talking. And the hands of the big clock move slowly, slowly.

ROSA. They can always kill us if they want to.

COATES. But Fritz does manage to slip out of the country, and settles in Hollywood, where he discovers that if you play your cards right, you don't actually have to finish anything. Just bring in a new draft every six months and pretend to listen to some cigar chomping ignoramus puke out a bunch of rubbish and go home and do a couple of rewrites and bring it back and listen to the same moron criticizing the changes he told you to make, and you can stay on the payroll forever.

NATASHA. Film lasts longer than memory.

COATES. You can live a very comfortable life if you just don't say no to these people. Just smile and nod and take their money. This is the only rule in Hollywood. Always take the money. Enjoy the orchestra playing while the ship is going down. So Fritz Lang spends the rest of his life beside his swimming pool, with his eyepatch and his stuffed monkey, manufacturing garbage. The one thing that never changes is that, both in his previous life, as an artist, and his subsequent life, as a prostitute, the actors all hate him. The crew hates him. Sand bags keep dropping and just missing him. No matter where you go or what you do, the lunatic in your head comes with you.

MULLIGAN. The point of all this being what?

COATES. The point of all this being, before he left Berlin, he murdered his wife. In a bath tub. Fritz Lang. That's the rumor, anyway. That was my inspiration. But who can blame Fritz Lang? It's our job to murder the people who love us. Otherwise, we might be in danger of actually loving them back. And we can't have that, can we?

13.

Mad Cow Disease

ROSA. Do you love me?

COATES. Let me count the ways. I don't have enough digits. I'm going to have to take off my pants.

ROSA. Sometimes it feels like you're angry at me, for reasons I don't understand. You're smiling, but you're angry.

COATES. The secret of getting women is to be a charming bastard.

ROSA. It's almost like you want to hit me.

COATES. And yet I restrain myself. I have the British public school to thank for my good breeding. There a young gentleman learns to display courtesy towards women while feeling them up under the table. And surreptitious buggering.

ROSA. Sometimes it feels almost as if you'd like to kill me.

COATES. All seducers hate women. That's why we work in the dark and always keep moving.

(Pause. He looks at her, sees the pain on her face.)

I'm joking, you know. I'm an actor, like everybody else here. I'm capable of feeling honest human emotions, just incapable of expressing them, so I create a persona, the charming rogue. I hate myself a great deal more than I hate women, but I compensate for it with arrogance. You think I haven't been to analysis? I know myself inside and out, and I'm here to tell you, it doesn't do a damned bit of good, except to the doctor's bank account. You mustn't let me upset you. I'm really quite harmless. And I'm very fond of you. You're the girl of my dreams. And the only girl I'll ever want again. Cross my heart and hope to die. The sooner the better.

ROSA. I saw you.

COATES. You saw what?

ROSA. I saw you with Megan.

MEGAN. This is wrong, what we're doing.

COATES. If it wasn't, what would be the point?

MEGAN. But I don't like betraying people.

COATES. We were rehearsing.

ROSA. You had your hand up her dress.

COATES. We were improvising.

ROSA. You slept with her.

COATES. Actually, there was very little sleeping involved.

MEGAN. It was an accident.

ROSA. An accident? You mean he tripped and fell on you with his penis?

MEGAN. You said you were done with him.

ROSA. Yes. Because of Natasha.

MEGAN. But Natasha doesn't want him.

COATES. Natasha wants me. She just doesn't want to sleep with me. At least, she doesn't know she wants to sleep with me. Or she knows she wants to sleep with me, and it terrifies her. Which is very upsetting for a sensitive person like myself. And you rejected me, after some seriously wonderful if tearful copulation. So who could blame me for accidentally falling on Megan with my penis?

MEGAN. I felt sorry for him. He's an idiot. And he's lonely.

ROSA. He's not lonely. He's a predatory, worthless piece of garbage.

COATES. Every girl's dream. Just like Papa.

MEGAN. Then why do you care?

COATES. It's not my fault she let me. She could have said no.

ROSA. You're a horrible person.

COATES. On some days I am a rather horrible person. But on other days, I'm surprisingly decent.

ROSA. I thought you cared for me.

COATES. I care very much for you.

ROSA. So you fucked my best friend?

COATES. In my country, it's traditional. Like having a Yule log. Or mad cow disease.

ROSA. I hate you.

COATES. If you hated me you wouldn't give a damn who I sleep with. Do you ever get the impression someone else has written the dialogue you hear coming out of your mouth? What is that thing moving across the carpet? There. Do you see that? The monkey runs along the wall. It follows me. I'm seeing things. Too much green tea. Clearly more alcohol is the answer.

(**COATES** *pours himself another drink.*)

14.

A Labyrinth Of Mirrors

NATASHA. Great. Now Rosa's upset, Megan's upset, and we're a month behind schedule. Must you deflower every single woman within a ten mile radius?

COATES. No. Some of them are married.

EMILIA. This man would fornicate with a crash dummy.

NATASHA. I know what men are like. I know you're compulsively on the hunt. I suppose you can't help it. But leave Rosa alone. You prey upon the innocent. You're very charming. You win them over. You use them up. And then you move on. You should probably be killed.

COATES. I've never met an innocent woman in my life. And do you really think you can keep me all to yourself and never let me touch you? That I'll be happy to cut off my testicles so you can hang them round your neck like a string of pearls? What do you want from me?

NATASHA. What I want, you can't give me.

COATES. And yet you can't seem to keep away from me. Russian sado-masochism. You people love to suffer, and you love to make others suffer, and then you all get together and cry about it, make crude jokes and say horrible things about the rest of us. You are a very sick person from a very sick nation which has inexplicably produced the greatest body of literature in the history of human futility, and I want to fornicate with you more than life itself. Take pity on me. I was up all night listening to you playing that damned piano. I should get something for that, shouldn't I?

(*To* **MULLIGAN**.)

This woman plays the piano like a monkey in boxing gloves. Even if she was ugly I'd sleep with her just to get her hands off the damned keyboard.

NATASHA. I play when I'm unhappy.

COATES. Well, you're certainly spreading the unhappiness around. That's what you do. You spread unhappiness like fertilizer in a desperate attempt to get rid of it. Doesn't work, though, does it? I admit I am not worthy of your love. I'm a cad, a bounder and a hack. I lie compulsively and I've wasted my talents manufacturing garbage for cretins. You could get someone better, both to write for you and to sleep with you, but the significant fact here is that you don't. A remarkably talented young woman, beautiful, strong and independent, and yet instead of kicking me out on my arse, as I deserve, you love me. You're frighteningly intelligent and yet unbelievably stupid. You give me no choice but to hurt you. You have cast me as the villain of the piece, and I'm just playing the part you've written for me.

NATASHA. You want her because she's younger.

COATES. I don't care about that.

NATASHA. Because she's more beautiful.

COATES. Nobody is more beautiful than you.

NATASHA. Why then?

COATES. Because you won't sleep with me.

NATASHA. But if I did sleep with you, you'd still betray me.

COATES. Of course I'd betray you. This is not the movies. In real life, people get what they want, get bored and move on.

NATASHA. I don't.

COATES. I know you don't. So it's my job. Somebody's got to do it. The person who doesn't move along first is the one who gets hurt. We must learn from our mistakes, although in point of fact we almost never do, and it is always a mistake to love. Love is always fatal. That's why when it takes up residence in one's soul one must exterminate it as soon as possible, like rats. Don't they teach you these things in Russia?

NATASHA. You're going to leave Rosa alone. Is that clear?

COATES. No, I don't think so.

EMILIA. Hell is murky.

NATASHA. You leave her alone or, trust me, you'll be sorry.

COATES. I don't trust you, and I'm already about as sorry a specimen as you're ever likely to meet. But I'm not as sick as you. Because you use people, too. You use movies to control people, and to hide in, like an elaborately fabricated labyrinth of mirrors. To tell you the truth, and I do that as seldom as possible, I've been having some serious concerns about your mental condition. I think you're beginning to suffer from delusions. Of course, you make movies, so your life is entirely constructed of delusions, but you can control what happens in your movies. In life, not so much. I really think there's something seriously wrong with you.

NATASHA. You're mounting every woman in sight and there's something wrong with me?

COATES. What else do I have? I am trapped in that circle of Hell reserved for bad Chinese food and unrequited love.

NATASHA. You've never loved anybody in your life.

COATES. Not true. I loved my first wife with the pathetic devotion of the mentally impaired. Came home one afternoon to find her in bed with a man wearing a raccoon hat. She said she could explain. Her explanation was that the raccoon hat was a part of his cultural tradition. My subsequent experiences with women have only confirmed that the world is made of betrayal and all love is self delusion. One must simply take whatever one wants, whenever one can get it, because everyone you think you love is just a glass of wine or two away from being repeatedly violated in the buttocks by a man with a dead animal on his head. Why have I come to this wilderness?

NATASHA. I don't actually love you any more. I thought I did once, for a short time, but now I don't. It's such an odd thing. A person wakes up one morning and looks at someone and suddenly, for the first time, she can see him as he actually is, and after so much pointless anguish, realizes she feels nothing. How could I love you? You're a walking corpse. What a waste of time it is to love a dead man.

COATES. *I Loved A Zombie.* One of my better screenplays, actually. About a woman who takes erotic pleasure from eating men alive. Or perhaps being eaten alive. I forget.

ROSA. I dream that I'm lost in the forest, stumbling over the roots of ancient trees. There are many strange lights. Monstrous creatures lurk here. There is evil in this place.

NATASHA. If you touch her again, I'll kill you.

COATES. No. You're more likely to kill her. We usually find a way to murder those who love us. And if they're stupid enough to love us, they probably deserve it.

15.

Somebody Who's Making A Movie

EMILIA. You try to keep Coates away from her, and you tell yourself it's for her own good, but you're doing more harm to her than he is. You're hurting that child.

NATASHA. I'm not hurting her. I saved her. I gave her a life.

EMILIA. You're using her.

NATASHA. I'm not using her.

EMILIA. You use everything. And everybody.

NATASHA. Do you think I've used you?

EMILIA. Of course you have.

NATASHA. I'm including you in my life. I'm putting you in the movie.

EMILIA. I don't want to be in the damned movie.

NATASHA. Then what do you want?

EMILIA. Not this. Not anything like this. I want it to be like it was before.

NATASHA. Before what?

EMILIA. The snow was falling, and everything was silent, and you were so beautiful. You were trying to die, and I saved you.

NATASHA. And you're never going to let me forget it.

EMILIA. Before you retreated into movies and never came out. You can't hide in the art you make. The real world is still out there all around you and sooner or later it comes to get you. And you don't know anything about the real world.

NATASHA. Movies exist in the real world. They do things to people. They make money. They make us famous. They give us power. When you've been powerless all your life, you learn to value power.

EMILIA. And then you start using it to destroy the people around you.

NATASHA. Tell me how I'm hurting her.

EMILIA. You're trying to make her into somebody she's not.

NATASHA. Well, she doesn't want to be who she is. That's what movies are for. They give us a chance to be somebody else.

EMILIA. Really? And who are you?

NATASHA. I'm somebody who's making a movie.

EMILIA. At the expense of your own soul, and the happiness of everybody else. You enjoy so much playing the role of the great director, but you're actually a sadist pretending to be an artist. And look inside a sadist and you find a masochist. There is something inside you that worships pain. Your pain and other people's. And the innocent and the vulnerable bring this out in you. You think you want to protect them, but you end up destroying them, because you're afraid of the pain they can cause you, so you use them up and then you get rid of them.

NATASHA. I'm not getting rid of anybody.

EMILIA. Just everybody who loves you. You treat people like you were editing a film. Use what you need. Throw out the rest.

NATASHA. Sometimes you need to be cruel for the sake of art.

EMILIA. Yes, you go right on telling yourself that. Just remember that at some point the movie ends, and then what are you going to do?

NATASHA. Make another one.

COATES. Fear death by water.

16.

Everywhere There Are Spirits

ROSA. I love how the bubbles feel on my skin. Naked in warm liquid is our natural state. It's what we remember when we sleep. It's the movie running in our heads just before we come out screaming, blinded by projected light. There are little motes of dust floating in the light, each one a universe. This movie is a dream.

EMILIA. You don't live in a movie. You are a movie.

ROSA. I dozed off for a moment, and dreamed that my father came to me and warned me. He said I was in danger.

COATES. Rosa? Are you all right in there?

ROSA. Everywhere there are spirits. They are all around us.

COATES. Rosa?

MEGAN. You said you never knew your father.

ROSA. Maybe it wasn't my father. Maybe it was somebody else's father. There were a lot of ticking clocks, and it was snowing. Maybe it was some sort of policeman. A sad man with an Irish name. He was looking for his daughter, but she was lost at sea.

COATES. I'm coming in.

ROSA. You stay out of here. I mean it. I've got a gun.

COATES. You don't have a gun.

ROSA. I could have a gun.

COATES. You need to come out of there, right now, or Natasha will be very angry at you, and we don't want Natasha to get angry, do we?

ROSA. In my dream, the hands of the clock tower move towards midnight. The gravedigger's daughter sits in the walled garden, knitting sweaters for dead actors. Like one of the Fates. Demons are creeping about in the darkness. Spiders in her head. The policeman who is not her father is trying to save her, but he's too late. You can't save the dead.

MEGAN. You know what you're doing with Coates, don't you? You're looking for a father. That's why you allow yourself to be violated by a pig like that. He's just a poor substitute for what you really want. Or think you want. Well, I've had a father, and, let me tell you, sometimes a girl is better off without. My old Dad used to beat the living daylights out of us with his fists and sometimes a belt. You could hear the screaming all over Dublin. He beat Mum, he beat the boys, he beat the girls. He beat the big ones and he beat the little ones. He didn't play favorites. He was an equal opportunity son of a bitch. I got the hell out of there when I was sixteen, and I don't miss it, not ever, not for one second.

ROSA. But you've slept with him, too. You're sleeping with Coates now.

COATES. I'll stop her throat with winter plums.

MEGAN. So? What's your point?

ROSA. So you're looking for a father, too.

MEGAN. I'm not looking for anything.

ROSA. Then why are you doing it?

MEGAN. Because I'm not looking for anything.

COATES. Eyes of the monkey. Two red eyes in the dark.

NATASHA. My father's eyes.

MEGAN. Now, Natasha—she's looking for something.

ROSA. What is it?

MEGAN. Something she can't have.

17.

Casablanca

NATASHA. In the dark house with many rooms there is a lost child. Moonlight streams through the half-opened window. There's a dark figure by the bed, staring down at me, with two red eyes. Someone is sobbing in another room. It's all smoke and mirrors. My father repaired clocks. We lived above the shop. At night I'd be in bed with the clocks all ticking and chiming, listening for my mother to come home. I knew he was listening too. Sometimes it would rain and storm. I was born in a thunderstorm. My mother almost died, and she was never the same after, my father said. Something went wrong in her head. He blamed me for it. He loved her past all reason. But she never would let him touch her after that. Then she began sneaking out at night. It is dangerous to love too much. It is dangerous to love at all. Is the script different?

COATES. Nothing is different. I'm telling you, you're going insane. Of course, this is the movie business. Everybody we know is insane. Sane people make automatic weapons and bombs. What I want to know is, why do we need to do so many damned takes? You'd think we were making the greatest movie since *Casablanca*.

NATASHA. *Casablanca* is a stupid movie. It doesn't make any sense. People don't give people up for love or political causes. They give them up because they don't want them.

EMILIA. She compulsively reworks the material again and again. Pieces of it appear and disappear in different variations and combinations. She does this not to find the truth but to conceal it in a multitude of false pathways. The liar and the artist are the same, like the saved and the damned. Both prefer alternate versions of reality. Movies are lies preserved and shareable. They're the time travel of lying.

NATASHA. I work this way because I don't trust anything that's all tied up in a neat bundle. In art or in life. When everything is working perfectly I grow uneasy. Disorder is what reminds you you're alive. The universe is random, but there is order. As in God's work of art, so in ours.

EMILIA. God is like Alfred Hitchcock. He appears in all his movies, but if you don't pay attention, you'll miss him.

NATASHA. On the one hand, the impulse to control, to shape. On the other hand, the desire to just see what happens. A work of art is the product of both. To create a universe is to juggle order and disorder. To plan ahead but appreciate the random beauty that unexpectedly appears, and use it. The world is a collage. Structure is an illusion created by the ghosts of random events. Each random event is a dot. Our imaginations connect the dots, like finding animals in the constellations. But you could also draw the lines differently. You plan, but you remain open to the evolving flow of events, which is how one collaborates with God.

EMILIA. Or the Devil. How can you be sure you're not collaborating with the Devil? When I was a bad girl, which was often, the nuns would lock me in the closet with the Devil. The Devil is in there, they'd say. The Devil is in there with you in the dark. And I would huddle in the corner, terrified, trembling, peeing myself. To this day, I can tell when the Devil is near, because he smells like moth balls. While trapped in the closet in the dark the Devil explained to me what people were like, but I didn't believe him then, because he was the Prince of Lies. Now I know the Devil doesn't need to lie. He can do his work just fine by speaking the truth.

18.

Why Is A Raven Like A Writing Desk?

ROSA. Why do you watch me so much? You watch me over and over again. Why do you do that?

MULLIGAN. You put me in mind of my daughter.

ROSA. Is she dead?

MULLIGAN. Not that I know of.

ROSA. Then I'm not her.

MULLIGAN. No.

ROSA. So why are you staying up late, talking to a dead girl?

MULLIGAN. I'm trying to solve a puzzle.

ROSA. How is a raven like a writing desk?

MULLIGAN. How you died.

ROSA. I drowned. Those are pearls that were my eyes.

MULLIGAN. But why did you drown?

ROSA. Too much water. Not enough air. Everything in your life is either too much or not enough, and the line between is very thinly drawn.

MULLIGAN. Somebody killed you. Who was it?

MEGAN. Mulligan?

MULLIGAN. What?

MEGAN. Talking to yourself, are you?

MULLIGAN. Nobody else will listen.

MEGAN. I have something to tell you.

MULLIGAN. Are you here to confess?

MEGAN. Only if there's a priest.

MULLIGAN. My mother wanted me to be a priest, but that was never a serious option after I saw my cousin Mary naked. Mom never forgave me. She hated being married to a cop. Can't say I blame her. My wife didn't like it much, either.

MEGAN. But you didn't just have those two choices, cop or priest. There were other things you could have done.

MULLIGAN. I don't know. The look in my father's eyes, when I told him. Sad, but proud of me. That was worth it. You know the look I mean?

MEGAN. No. I don't.

MULLIGAN. What did you want to tell me?

MEGAN. You asked me who Valentina was. The girl Rosa kept talking about when she called me, and I remembered something. She actually mentioned that name once before, maybe a month or so before she died. Rosa told me that one night, not long after she'd first moved into the brownstone with us, there was a big thunderstorm. Rosa was terrified of thunderstorms. And she was alone in her room in this strange building and decided to come and look for me, but she got the rooms mixed up, and she called out my name, in the hallway, and she heard somebody say something in one of the rooms, and thought it was me answering her, so she went in, and it was Natasha's bedroom. And Natasha was all twisted up in the covers, having a nightmare of some sort, and crying, and speaking in Russian, so of course Rosa had no idea what she was saying, except she kept repeating the name Valentina. Rosa knew she should just get out of there, but she said Natasha looked so beautiful, lying there naked in the moonlight and crying, and talking in her sleep, and saying this name, that for a long time she just stood there and stared at her. Like she was paralyzed. And she had this overwhelming desire to crawl into bed with her, and comfort her, but then she heard somebody coming up the steps, so she went back to her room.

MULLIGAN. And she never asked Natasha about it?

MEGAN. No. She was too embarrassed. Does that help?

MULLIGAN. Yes it does. Thank you.

MEGAN. Are you okay?

MULLIGAN. I don't know. Sure. Why?

MEGAN. I've been smelling liquor on your breath.

MULLIGAN. I'm all right.

MEGAN. Are you missing your daughter?

MULLIGAN. I'm fine.

MEGAN. Do you want company?

MULLIGAN. No.

MEGAN. Are you sure?

MULLIGAN. No. Yes. I'm sure. No. Go to bed.

MEGAN. Okay.

(**MEGAN** *hesitates, then turns and goes.*)

ROSA. You're getting too close.

MULLIGAN. Too close to what?

ROSA. To everything. Watch out. I have this dream that I'm lying naked in the water, looking up. Somebody has sucked out my soul and there's nothing left inside me. I'm completely empty.

MULLIGAN. Who killed you, Rosa?

ROSA. Valentina. Valentina killed me.

19.

Through A Glass Darkly

NATASHA. You're still here. Why are you still here?

MULLIGAN. I'm trying to figure you people out, but the more I learn the less I'm sure about. It's like you're all from some other planet.

NATASHA. We're more alike than you want to admit. Making a movie is like putting together a puzzle. It's an investigation. An attempt to understand something, even if you're not sure what it is you're trying to understand. To find an explanation whether there is one or not. We're both in the business of constructing hypothetical realities.

MULLIGAN. I'm not constructing anything. I'm looking for the truth.

NATASHA. No, you're inventing a story that seems to fit and trying to make the rest of us accept it as reality. But the explanation you come up with is always a lie because an explanation is a hypothetical construction, which by definition is a lie. I grew up in the Soviet Union, I'm an expert on this. A movie is like a reflection in a dark mirror. It's not the real thing, and the same object looks different in different mirrors and under different light, but art admits this. You don't. Your truth is hypocrisy because it perpetuates the lie that truth is knowable. It's the hypocrisy of law, of authority, of violence. Of course, when a work of art tries to reflect that violence, it runs the risk of becoming an act of violence itself. Art is more dangerous than you think. But what I do is more honest than what you do.

ROSA. At the orphanage they told us: the bad children we put in a bag and drown.

MULLIGAN. There's a dead girl here, and she's real, and there's a reason she's dead, and I'm going to find it.

NATASHA. Actually you're not, because we're replacing you.

MULLIGAN. Replacing me?

NATASHA. We've decided to recast the role of the police detective. We appreciate very much the contributions you've made, but it just isn't working out.

MULLIGAN. I don't understand.

NATASHA. We feel that your character has become too emotionally involved. At first it was kind of exciting, watching him getting pulled deeper and deeper into what was for him a kind of alternate universe, but as he got more and more attached, we felt that he became less and less credible. So we're going in another direction.

MULLIGAN. You can't replace me.

NATASHA. I can do anything I want. I'm the director. This is my world and I'm God here. But we sincerely wish you the very best of luck in all future projects.

MULLIGAN. Coates is right. You're not well.

NATASHA. Of course I'm not well. I haven't been well for some time. I have been dancing just at the edge of the abyss for several years now. But I have excellent balance. I've been a dancer since I was a child. In my head, I'm still dancing. Just at the edge.

MULLIGAN. Tell me what happened to that girl.

NATASHA. I don't know what happened to her.

MULLIGAN. She didn't kill herself and it wasn't any accident. Did you find her with Coates? Is that how it was? You came in out of the snow and found them together, and that's what set you off? Is he lying to protect you?

COATES. Silence. Exile. Cunning.

MULLIGAN. You came in out of the snow and found them in the bathroom, her naked in the tub—maybe both of them in the tub.

NATASHA. That's not true. She was only half naked. And she wasn't in the tub. They were on the sofa. And it wasn't the day she died. It was the day before.

ROSA. He was helping me rehearse a scene.

NATASHA. Without your shirt?

ROSA. It was warm in here.

NATASHA. There are icicles hanging from the gutters. Birds are stuck to trees. Small children are throwing frozen rats against buildings and watching them shatter like glass. And you're sitting in the parlor with your tits out because it's too warm in here?

ROSA. I'm sorry.

NATASHA. It's not your fault. It's him. Can't you see what a shit he is? He's a monster.

COATES. You like to think so because that's why you can't resist me. You're attracted to monsters. My guess is that your father was a monster.

NATASHA. You don't know anything about my father.

COATES. I don't know anything about anybody. But I'm right, though, aren't I?

EMILIA. My father used to take out his glass eye, put it in the olive dish, and say "Here's looking at you, kid."

MULLIGAN. So you found Coates and Rosa half undressed on the sofa, and what did you do?

NATASHA. I told her to stay away from him. She stormed out. We had a difficult time on the set the next day. She was exhausted. She went home to rest, and I came back and found her dead.

MULLIGAN. You're lying.

NATASHA. I'm not lying.

MULLIGAN. You've got a tell. You blink when you're lying.

NATASHA. I don't blink when I'm lying.

　　　(She blinks.)

All right. The second time she was dead. I was there twice. When I left the first time, she was alive. I didn't tell you because it didn't seem to matter.

MULLIGAN. You didn't tell me because something happened you didn't want me to know about. What happened?

NATASHA. She was upset. She wanted to leave the film.

20.

A Language I Don't Speak

ROSA. I don't think I can do this any more.

NATASHA. Of course you can. Come back to the set now. We need you.

ROSA. It's too much for me. I can't eat. I can't sleep. I can't sit still. I can't concentrate. It's destroying me. This is the only place I can relax.

NATASHA. But you're not relaxed. Look at all the tension in your shoulders. Here.

(**NATASHA** *begins to massage her shoulders.*)

You're full of knots. There. And there. And there. If you want to be an actress, you need to learn how to relax. If you can't relax, you can't be strong, and you've got to be strong to do this.

ROSA. Sometimes I'm strong. I could be strong. But it's so horribly lonely here. Everything here is a game. Everything is a lie. And everybody here is using everybody else. It's like I'm being translated into a language I don't speak. I think in some other life I used to be somebody else, somebody happier, but I can't quite remember. In the subway, I had this overwhelming impulse to throw myself in front of an oncoming train, like Anna Karenina.

NATASHA. You just need to stay away from Coates. He's polluting your soul. People like that are poison.

ROSA. I know he's a terrible person, but while he was chasing after me, I felt wanted. Like somebody needed something from me. I could at least perpetuate for a while the illusion that I was loved. And even now, when I look at him, something from the past reaches into my soul like a giant claw and squeezes until I can't breathe, and I want that feeling back.

NATASHA. We never get over anything. In our souls we're always making the same movie. We just recast the roles.

ROSA. That feels so good. At one of the foster homes I grew up in, there was an older girl who would give me massages. The only place I felt safe there was in their big old claw-foot tub. And she would touch me. So gently. So tenderly. Once she kissed me. It might have been the only time in my life I was ever completely happy. Just that moment. But she never did it again.

NATASHA. *(Kneeling by the tub, her face level with* ROSA*'s, putting her hand on* ROSA*'s cheek.)* Look at me. Nobody here is going to hurt you, because I am not going to let that happen. I'll protect you. I swear I will. But you need to come back to the set. That's where you belong. You're safe here. You have a home with us.

> *(A moment.* ROSA *puts her hand on* NATASHA*'s cheek and then kisses her.* EMILIA *enters.)*

EMILIA. Somebody's missing from my doll house. I think one of the rats ate her.

> *(*EMILIA *sees them.)*

What is this? What the hell is this? This is what you do? You rescue this poor child so you can molest her in the bathtub?

NATASHA. Nobody is molesting anybody. And in any case, it's none of your business.

EMILIA. None of my business? It's none of my business? Who are you to tell me what is and isn't my business? You're only here because of me. You're alive because of me. You were freezing to death and I rescued you. You were starving to death and I fed you. And now I find out you're some sort of a child molester.

NATASHA. She's not a child and I didn't molest her.

ROSA. She didn't do anything.

EMILIA. You stay out of this.

ROSA. It was me. Not her.

EMILIA. I've done everything for you. You had nothing, and I gave you everything. And you behave like I'm your servant. I have loved you so much. And you treat me with such contempt.

NATASHA. I don't treat you with contempt. I just can't love you the way you want me to. I can't love anybody. I could once. I can't any more. Something has died in me. I'm only happy in the dark. To sit in the dark and be so lost you are somehow comforted, or at least too occupied, for the moment, to cut your throat. That's all I have.

EMILIA. I should have left you in the snow.

　　　(EMILIA *goes.*)

ROSA. It's all my fault. I didn't mean to cause any trouble.

NATASHA. It's not your fault. She's had too much to drink. I'll talk to her. She'll be fine.

ROSA. Nobody is going to be fine. That's some other movie. Not this one. This is a different movie altogether.

21.

The Queen Of The Rainy Country

NATASHA. I went after Emilia, but I couldn't find her. And when I came back, I found Rosa dead.

MULLIGAN. There's something else.

NATASHA. There's nothing else. I've told you everything.

MULLIGAN. Something you know, or something you suspect, or something you don't realize you know. You're leaving something out.

NATASHA. You keep telling yourself you can understand what happened, or why it happened. But the past is just a movie in your head. That's the only place it exists. The truth is what you can deal with.

MULLIGAN. No. There is a reality separate from what you want, separate from what you fear, and separate from the movie you make in your head. And it is possible to comprehend it.

NATASHA. It's not possible to comprehend anything or anybody. The heart of another is a dark forest. Russian proverb.

ROSA. Valentina. It's a name she says in her sleep. And she cries.

MULLIGAN. Who is Valentina?

NATASHA. Nobody.

MULLIGAN. Just before she died, she called Megan on the phone, and asked for somebody named Valentina. Who is Valentina?

NATASHA. This has nothing to do with what happened here.

MULLIGAN. I think it does. I think there's something inside you that if I can understand it, I can understand what happened. It's somebody who haunts you. You say her name in your sleep.

NATASHA. How the hell do you know what I say in my sleep?

MULLIGAN. Who is Valentina?

NATASHA. I'm cutting this scene. This is not in the movie.

MULLIGAN. No. This scene is in the movie. This is the movie.

NATASHA. The movie is what I say it is.

MULLIGAN. Except for this part. This is the part God collaborates on. The part you can't control.

EMILIA. When God collaborates, somebody always dies.

NATASHA. I don't think it's God. Maybe Emilia is right. Maybe it's the Devil I'm collaborating with. I'm not even sure I know what's real any more.

MULLIGAN. Who is Valentina?

NATASHA. After my mother left, it was just me and Papa. I would sit at her piano and play Chopin, and try to get lost in the music.

> (*Sound of the Chopin Prelude, playing softly, as at the beginning.*)

I would never have harmed that girl. She was like a child to me.

MULLIGAN. Who is Valentina?

NATASHA. My child.

MULLIGAN. Your child?

NATASHA. I had a child. I named her Valentina, after my mother. She was gone, and my father started drinking, and I went a bit wild. I was a very promiscuous teenage girl. I wasn't even sure who the father was. And it really didn't matter to me. She was all that mattered. I wanted somebody to love. She was everything to me. My father said I was a whore like my mother. But I didn't care. I had my child.

> (*The various instruments begin to join in, to create the growing practice rooms cacophony, as before.*)

But after she was born, he got worse and worse. He was drinking and wandering around the house at night, having long conversations with my mother, who wasn't there. Screaming at her. Throwing things. One night he went out to the shed and got an ax, and destroyed the the piano.

(Sound of the ax destroying the piano. Then silence.)

That was when I knew I had to get my child out of that place.

MULLIGAN. Where is she now?

NATASHA. She died.

MULLIGAN. How did she die?

NATASHA. She died, and I went to Berlin, to start a new life.

MULLIGAN. What happened to your child?

NATASHA. I knew my father would never let me leave. She abandoned him. Now I was abandoning him. He'd never have accepted it.

MULLIGAN. How did your child die?

NATASHA. She drowned. In her bath.

MULLIGAN. Did you drown her?

NATASHA. No.

MULLIGAN. You drowned your child so you could go to Berlin and be a dancer.

NATASHA. No.

MULLIGAN. You drowned your child, and Rosa was like your child, and when she threatened to abandon you, like your mother did, you drowned her, too.

NATASHA. I did not drown my child. I loved my child. I would never hurt my child. I would die for my child.

MULLIGAN. Then you were careless. You were careless and she drowned.

NATASHA. I was not careless.

MULLIGAN. Then what happened to her? How did she drown?

(Faint sound of clocks ticking, and of water dripping.)

NATASHA. I was leaving for Berlin that night. I'd made all the arrangements. I just had to pick up my passport. There was nobody to watch her. I just left her alone for a half hour. She was sleeping, in her cradle, very peacefully. My father was out drinking somewhere. I had to get the passport. I didn't want to wake her up and take her out in the cold. I had very little time. My father would never have let me go, so I kept it from him. But he found out somehow. And he was very angry. He was very, very angry. He was a gentle person, ordinarily. But after he started drinking, after my mother left, he had a violent temper. And I came home. And the house was quiet. All I could hear was the ticking of my father's clocks, and the sound of water dripping upstairs. And I knew something was wrong. And I ran up the steps. And I found my child in the tub. I pulled her out of the water, and I tried to revive her, but she wasn't breathing. And my father was standing there in the doorway, and I screamed at him to call an ambulance, but he just stood there and looked at me, and he said, now you know what it feels like, to lose everything you love. So I picked up the iron. And I hit him in the head. I don't know how many times I hit him. And then I gathered my child up in a blanket and I ran out into the street with her and flagged down a car and took her to the hospital, but she was gone.

MULLIGAN. And your father?

NATASHA. I don't know. I don't know to this day if he's living or dead. And I don't care. I walked out of the hospital and I went to the airport, half insane with grief, but numb, increasingly numb, in a kind of trance, like in a dream, and I got on the plane and went to Berlin. But there was nothing for me there. No work. No money. No food. Nothing. And I went to that one last audition, but when I got to the top floor, where the practice rooms were, and I heard the sound of all that music, all jumbled together, it was like the sound of my father chopping up my mother's piano, and I ran back down the steps and into the street, and it had begun to snow. And when I saw the snow, I thought of my child, and I sat down on the sidewalk, with my back to the wall, in the snow, and I covered my face, and I wanted to die.

(Pause. The ticking clock and dripping sound have faded.)

But Emilia saved me. And she introduced me to this other world, where I could escape from these memories for a while. Except there is no escape. It's always there. You never get rid of it. And it gets into your work. No matter how hard you try to keep it out, everything that has ripped your guts out gets into your work, one way or another, so maybe you can turn it into something else and share it with somebody and it doesn't hurt so bad, but the pain never goes away. And when I saw Rosa, when I looked into her eyes, I saw my child. She had the face of my child. And I wanted to save her. So I took her in. But she didn't like it. She didn't want it. She just wanted to get away.

MULLIGAN. She was going to abandon you. Like your mother abandoned you. She was going to betray you the way your mother betrayed your father. And you felt just like he did. So you did to her what your father did to your child.

NATASHA. No.

MULLIGAN. You drowned Rosa like your father drowned your child.

NATASHA. I didn't drown her. I didn't. I came back and found her. I swear. When I found her, it was like a nightmare. It was like my child all over again. I held her in my arms and I couldn't stop screaming. How cruel does God have to be to prove he doesn't exist? And Emilia found me. And she comforted me while we waited for the ambulance and the police. She was very tender and loving to me. And by the time they came, I was numb again.

(Pause.)

MULLIGAN. Who else knew?

NATASHA. Who else knew what?

MULLIGAN. Who else knew about your child?

NATASHA. Nobody.

MULLIGAN. Nobody else knew what happened to your child?

NATASHA. I never told anybody. Just Emilia.

EMILIA. Objects are alive.

MULLIGAN. Emilia knew?

EMILIA. Everything in a movie is alive.

NATASHA. That first night. In Berlin. It was snowing, and it was so cold. There was only the one bed. And we were cuddled up in her bed together, for warmth. And I was so unhappy. I'd been so alone. She held me. And I cried. And I told her. And she comforted me. She's the only person I ever told. I never mentioned it again. Why is that important?

COATES. Fear death by water.

NATASHA. (*Looking across the stage, where* **EMILIA** *is standing behind the tub, looking at* **ROSA**.) Oh, my god.

22.

God's Memory

ROSA. She's gone out to look for you. Did you see her?

EMILIA. No.

ROSA. I'm so sorry about everything. It was all my fault. It was just—

EMILIA. It's all right.

ROSA. I didn't mean to hurt anybody.

EMILIA. I know.

ROSA. I'm getting so sleepy. I just want to go to sleep.

EMILIA. *(Putting her hands on **ROSA**'s shoulders.)* It's all right, child. Go to sleep. The world will still be here when you wake up. It's all like a movie. Objects are alive. Everything in a movie is alive. All things are full of gods. There are spirits everywhere, all around us. We are just God's memory, playing again and again like a movie in his head. We're all just toys in his doll house.

NATASHA. *(Center stage, as at the beginning.)* None of this is real.

ROSA. I was just lonely.

NATASHA. They're all just characters in a movie.

> *(From this point on, gradually increasing, the flickering of the lights, as in an old movie, and the faint sound of film moving through a projector.)*

EMILIA. I know, child. Just to be connected to something, some warm, living creature.

NATASHA. The only thing real is suffering.

EMILIA. And yet that is the cause of all suffering, the passion to connect, and the betrayal and rejection that inevitably follows.

NATASHA. I've conjured up this movie to hide in, from the pain.

EMILIA. The Devil is always sneaking into the kitchen at night and poisoning the sauce. At the center of Hell, his great wings beat like a windmill.

NATASHA. You are all just happening in my head as I sit in the snow on a street in Berlin.

EMILIA. Everything will be all right.

NATASHA. No one comes to rescue me.

EMILIA. And if you don't wake up, she can never hurt you again, like she hurt me.

ROSA. I'm falling asleep.

EMILIA. Like she hurts everybody.

NATASHA. Numbness slowly creeping up my body.

EMILIA. The wreckage of her victims is strewn about in the ice, twisted grotesquely in their agony.

NATASHA. Death, like a lover.

EMILIA. All the rivers of guilt flow here.

NATASHA. It's like drowning.

EMILIA. And when she returns, and finds you, oh, what a nice surprise it will be for her. What a nice surprise. And I will comfort her.

> *(Sound of the film flying off the end of the reel and flapping as* **EMILIA** *begins to slowly push* **ROSA** *down into the water. The light fades on them and goes out. In the darkness, the sound of the Chopin Prelude.)*

NOTEBOOK: A SNOWFALL IN BERLIN

The relationship between art and life blurs, imagination and reality. Life keeps bleeding into her art, the art into her life. To try and separate the two does not work, is not compatible with art, life, or sanity. And yet when the relationship between art and life blurs, imagination and reality can begin to blur, and that is another path to madness. How the two relate to one another, blend, separate, blend again, is something an artist deals with every day, consciously or unconsciously. In Natasha's case, she has created an artistic universe to hide in because the reality she is fleeing from was too monstrous for her to deal with. But whatever reality is, however strange and unreal it might seem, it always, in the end, comes to get you. Art is a place you can find comfort, but ultimately, you can't hide there.

On one level she looks at Rosa and sees herself. But on another level her obsession with Rosa is an attempt to recreate her relationship with the dead child. She is a deeply repressed person, and full of ambivalent feelings. She has a deep romantic attachment to Coates, but can't bear to let him touch her. She is very fond of and grateful to Emilia, but can't let her get too close. She envies Megan her more practical attitude towards relationships, but also finds it contemptible.

Invent yourself in the moment, she tells them. I am the movie. What matters is what you don't see. Nobody knows what's inside anybody else, and nobody knows what's inside themselves. Nobody knows what they can or can't do. Create or destroy. Love or hate. There are strangers inside you. Do not analyze. Do not explain. Let it be what it is.

When an image comes into contact with other images, a chemical reaction occurs. It is a kind of alchemy. Sometimes it's like this with people. Sex happens, or murder, or both. Art is perpetual transformation.

You keep turning into different people so nobody will find out who you are. Or so you won't.

Sometimes a look tells you everything. You don't want to know, but you can't look away. Sometimes you don't understand a look at first, but then later, months or years later, you remember that look, and you understand what it meant. But then it's too late. We live life forwards, but we can only understand it backwards.

She creates an environment which intensifies a person's inherent lunacy. It bubbles up from the deepest and most secret penetralia of her soul. The penetralia, the innermost parts, as of a building, a secret or hidden place, innermost things.

In this play we are often seeing one thing and hearing another. Other times and places are superimposed upon the apparent present, and the present, once the future, is always now the past. You can't hold onto it. It squirms out of your grasp like a wet mermaid.

Infinite depth, rich complexity, ambiguity and mystery. Reality seems uncanny: in Freud's terms, something once known, then repressed, bobbing unexpectedly to the surface is what produces the feeling of the uncanny, and makes the hair stand up on the back of our necks. This is what art is for. Art is made of that thing bobbing to the surface, and it exists to lure such things to the surface in others. When it works right, it fills one with that ominous, uncanny sense that a strange god is present.

Eisenstein called art a clash of opposing passions, lying at the intersection of nature (the organic) and industry (the manufactured). That is, the intersection of the irrational inside us and our powerful compulsion to explain the world rationally and perceive form. For Eisenstein, it is this dialectic conflict from which the power of art is generated.

Eisenstein's chains of psychological association. The juxtaposition of disparate events. A montage is an accumulation of associations. Somehow, the act of presenting in fragments multiplies the emotional charge.

A play that is a kind of associational montage. When being chased by a cow through an emotional field, watch where you step.

On the one hand, the movie is a dream structure we are trapped in, like rats in a maze. On the other hand, we are free to trace our own paths through the maze. The path we trace in the maze is our free will. The maze itself is the determinism of the given circumstances.

Even if we are unable to comprehend it, we must at least find a way to perceive the beauty in the apparent disorder which surrounds us, or go mad. One attempts, in writing, Salinger said, to relax and tap into the poetry that flows through all things.

What we are seeing could be what Coates is writing, or what Rosa is dreaming, or what Natasha is hallucinating as she freezes to death in the snow in Berlin. Or it could be the confused memory of a movie Megan saw once, or a drunken fantasy of Mulligan's as he mourns for his lost daughter's love. Or all or none of the above. We are constructed entirely of fragments of other people.

Love is an unfortunate series of arbitrary and false associations. When we think we have fallen in love with a person, what is really happening is that we are projecting upon them the qualities we miss from some earlier person we were under the illusion that we loved. Freud was right to trace these chains of association back to our childhood. But the paradox is that it's all we have. Love is something we think is real, discover is an illusion, but then embrace anyway, because there really is nothing else. Art that is not on some level an expression of love is meaningless.

That horrifying moment when you realize that the person you've been pretending to be turns out to be the person you've become.

Ironic and desperate contemplation. At random.

We could go to Greece and frolic naked in the rubble. The monkey runs along the wall. It follows me. Green tea.

Don't you hear something? Don't you hear something strange? Shuffling along just at the back of one's head? Rustling in the underbrush?

The associational nature of montage: meaning is derived not necessarily from the images themselves as from their association with other images in time and space.

How much, in a work of art, can one afford to leave to chance, given the inherent stupidity of the audience?

The ordering of images in time which is memory, constantly shuffled like a pack of cards. The Queen of Spades. The cat, Leopardi, at random, staring at nothing.

The lover's confession. Weaving a pattern of painful adventures. Unravelling a ball of twine. The beautiful lady without mercy. Strewn all around her lie the bones of her former lovers. I've spent my life between the bed and the window.

Borges says the four basic themes of imaginative fiction are the work inside a work, travel in time, the blending of dream and reality, and the double. All of these are present here.

In the courtyard the snow was falling heavily, the wind howled, the shutters shook and rattled. They descended into the garden.

She is the Queen of Spades. She has a great horror of drowned persons.

A confusion of voices. Pentecost. The tower of Babel.

Like certain water sprites, beautiful and compelling, but fated to bring unhappiness wherever she loves or is loved.

Mirrors have something monstrous about them. When someone dies, we cover the mirrors. The visible universe is an illusion. Mirrors are evil because they multiply that illusion.

The interesting thing is not that sometimes, during sex, I was tempted to put my hands around her throat and strangle her, but that she seemed to be excited by that prospect.

Something murky about the eyes. I look at her and I can hear the blood pounding in my ears.

Get thee to a nunnery.

When they throw stones at you, use them to build a labyrinth to hide in.

At every crossroads in the labyrinth, turn to your left.

My father said, when I was a baby, he showed me the moon, and I tried to reach up in the sky and grab it, like the Devil in the Gogol story.

She goes outside when it storms and stands in the rain. Lightning and thunder draw her. It's as if she's daring the lightning to strike her.

Two red eyes in the dark.

To replace one image with another is an act of violence. A film is the record of a series of murders of successive images. Much like the history of life. Life, like film is both the record of a process, and a process itself, and both are made of death.

Berlin drew me because it was broken and then put back together. I wanted that, too. To put myself back together. But when I got there I realized, even if the wall is torn down, the broken place remains.

In the mansion of shadows and images,
the attic is filled with birdcages,
and coagulated regrets.
And it always rains in your dreams.

Just after dark I come upon
the labyrinth of Babylon.
It's made of ancient cobblestones.
The corridors are strewn with bones.

Bath. Cleansing. Baptism. Water as life, death.

Bring me the head of John the Baptist. With pickles on the side.

What is this relentless strangeness? A set of Russian dolls, each universe nested inside another.

One should be totally enveloped by love, by a movie, by a play, like being swallowed by a great fish.

Mirrors reflecting mirrors. Which image is real? Multiple perspectives seen simultaneously. God's perspective. A collage of photographic negatives: Satan's perspective. Two sides of reality: creation and destruction.

Staring down into the East River. Trains roaring by in my head. The cars are being swallowed by the tunnel.

Drawn in by the relentless machinery of Hell. Just one fingertip in the machinery and you can be pulled in completely.

The play is a hall of mirrors reflecting mirrors. Rain as a unifying image. Tears. Urine. Menstrual blood. Semen. Release. Then it freezes. There is no more rain. It becomes cold and hard.

Polyphony, as in Palestrina, multiple lines played simultaneously. On the top floor of the music building, many rooms full of pianos. Many different pieces of music being rehearsed simultaneously. All the clocks say different times.

Film swallows up the audience. One is devoured by the film, becomes part of it, cannot escape it, like Jonah swallowed by the big fish, Ahab and the whale. It's hieroglyphics that move. Film is in your head.

Structure is the sequence of images in your head. If it seems random, it appears meaningless. But over-controlled, it seems false. How to unify the random nature of quantum reality with the obsessive need to find patterns so as to make sense of the world? It is not mere vanity. It is a matter of survival. What you don't think is real can kill you. Or, to put it another way, everything that can kill you is real.

Only people and gods can tell stories. We are the living dream iconography of an imaginary creator-god.

The succession of images. Simultaneous experience. Spatial continuity, time variation. Or the reverse. The order in which events occur is not the order in which we learn about them, which is not the same order in which we understand them.

What we remember is not what happened. What we think of as what happened is actually the memories we are able to reconstruct about what we were experiencing in our heads when we thought it was happening. Down the long, wet cobblestone hill to the deep well in which lurks the creature who will devour us. This is our life's journey.

A film, like a person's life, is put together out of fragments. We experience these fragments in one order. We remember them in another. Memory edits the film, along with desire and fear. Art changes your memory.

Hell, said Dostoyevsky, is the inability to love.

Everything is written in code. Everything we can touch is a symbol of something else. We spend our lives trying to reconstruct the lost code book. But the task is always left incomplete. The book is a palimpsest.

For the most part, now, I read to feed what I'm writing, and some of what I read has a direct, logical relationship to it. But something in me is also compulsively drawn to things that would appear to have no relationship whatsoever to what I'm writing, but my subconscious takes me there anyway, insistently, for reasons I will never understand, and, somehow, I find something there that feeds the particular strangeness of the work at hand. I have learned just to trust the madness and see where it takes me. It is at the intersection of roads you didn't think ever crossed, where the unexpected juxtaposition of disparate objects flowers into something uncanny. The uncanny, says Freud, is the reemergence of something we knew once, that has been deeply repressed. Something causes it to bob to the surface, and the hackles rise, goosebumps happen, we feel that strange thrill of oddness, the great god Pan suddenly perceived, moving through the ferns in the wind when everything else is still.

In my dreams they chase me through the catacombs. Monsters bulge out from the walls. I descend through a trap door and wade through a tunnel of sewage. And all for the love of the Queen of Iceland's daughter.

I just admitted to the moon
I don't know how to speak raccoon.
They have said that I'm insane,
just for dancing in the rain.
Melancholy reigns for miles
on the street of Crocodiles.

One observes from different angles. Vanishing apparitions.

Through the forest of dense mist, I wear my cloak of invisibility so my enemies can't find me. I am a genius at petrifying dwarfs. I studied dwarf petrification at Oxbridge. Laughter in the darkness of the park by the carnival. The organ grinder looks familiar. I have seen the murderer in the bushes. It is the duty of every mental patient to drive the psychiatrist mad. I loved a girl named Dementia Praecox. Carousel. Side shows. Freaks. A naked somnambulist told my fortune. A jagged, Gothic landscape.

I shall end up in a narrow house in a dark street off Piccadilly.

I am a clown dripping blood.

The future contained in the past like a seed.

Emilia reads Pirandello and weeps.

Only Americans wear raccoon hats. And only insane ones.

Emilia reads Pirandello and weeps for God's madness. She is afraid of bicycles and has erotic dreams about Fellini. Wet cobbles. A stranger takes her against a wall. No individual experience has any reality at all. Let us return to our sheep. An audience full of sheep. You are all dolls in my dollhouse.

It should be like music, with returning phrases and motifs. Like a revolving Greek chorus. The scenes have a core (the people who are there) and a chorus (the people who comment or are overheard but are perhaps not there). The key is to make it reasonably clear who is which in each scene, but not always certain what is real, or what real means in the context of this play.

Parallels, lines crossing the page from one character to another, images that reappear in different people's stories, deeply interwoven, labyrinthine, not willfully obscure, but never comprehended in their entirety. Like human experience, there is always something not understood.